Flirty

AT

MURPHY'S

A Murphy's Bar Novella

FRANKIE PAGE

DEDICATION

This story is dedicated to all those who have had a bad
Valentine's Day experience.

INTRODUCTION

Do you know what makes a great Valentine's Day? No, not a bunch of chocolates and flowers—those are for amateurs. Nope, the best way to celebrate Cupid's piss-poor aim... is by getting dumped. *Seriously, it's the greatest!* That way, you are freed up to go visit your favorite pub and tell good ol' Mr. Jameson all about your boy problems. What I didn't expect (you know, besides my ill-timed breakup) was a pair of panty-melting blue-green eyes strolling in and inserting themselves in the conversation. Eyes more intoxicating than the liquid filling my glass. It sure does make it a bit difficult to declare your hatred for all things male, when the alcohol isn't the only vice loosening your inhibitions. Yep, I'm dizzy all right, and it's not just 'cause of the whiskey. And, by all right, what I really mean is *all wrong*. It's way too fast. I seriously can't be falling in love with this mysterious fry thief... Can I?

Flirty at Murphy's is a standalone novella length romance complete with HEA, no cliffhanger, and no cheating. Note: this story is not suitable for persons under the age of 18. Potential triggers lie within this book.

CONTENTS

Anita

CHAPTER ONE

"I can't in good conscience give you another."
His tone, while stern, has a hint of sympathy.
Wordlessly, I point to the empty container.
He sighs, relents, and pours me another drink.
My thumb rubs the smooth surface of the glass
twice before I tighten my grip and lift it to my lips.

"Sean, we both know I haven't even begun to
hit my limit yet," I huff out. Guzzling down the
amber liquid, I welcome the comforting tingle as
it burns my throat. I slam the shot glass on the
wooden bar top, then use the lace sleeve of my
dress to wipe my mouth.

"Coming in here, and throwing back one too
many in celebration, before stumbling out with
your friend is one thing. This though..." He points
at my likely disheveled appearance. I don't dare
risk glancing behind him to look at my reflection.

No doubt my black liner and mascara are smudged under my watery eyes. "Let me call Tiffany."

"Don't," I interrupt him. "I don't want to ruin her night as well." I pull a crisp hundred from my wallet and lay it on the counter. "Leave me the bottle."

Sean eyes me for a second longer. Peering down the end of the bar, he seeks out his friend, and the owner of the establishment, Killian Murphy. The man in question leans up from the ledge, shifting his focus from flirting with the blonde in a skin-tight white dress—with way too much cleavage on display—and over to us. I glance down at my own attire, acknowledging that I'm no better, and shrug. I guess this is me being the proverbial pot. It's too loud in here to make out what he says, but knowing the Murphy brother for as long as I have, it's likely a string of curses. His gaze shifts from me to Sean. Killian drops his shoulders as he gives him a nod. Sean lets out an exhale, pushing the bottle closer to me.

"I'm bringing you a burger and fries." He stomps off as I pour myself another shot. In quick succession, I slam back two more mouthfuls. Finally, the god-awful Pepto-pink hearts and streamers fade into the blurry background. My stomach grumbles and twists into a knot. *Did I eat today?* No, that's right... I didn't. We were supposed to be going out to the Brazilian steakhouse tonight, and I didn't want to fill up beforehand. "Where's Sean? And that burger?" I grumble to myself. He's down at the end of the

2

bar, serving other patrons. A small bowl to my right catches my attention. I slide it closer. Upon further inspection, I see that it's filled with candy hearts. If their chalky texture wasn't enough to make me gag, surely the asinine sentiments engraved in sugar would do the trick. Desperate to put some form of food in my gut, I pick them up one by one, reading the false promises they offer.

Be mine.

Soul mate.

True love.

Forever.

I swallow each lie, between gritted teeth, hopefully saving another victim from their inevitable bait and switch. I go to reach for the next heart-shaped confectionary conspirator, except instead of digging my fingers into the bowl and feeling small candies, I run smack dab into something hard and warm. I attempt again, but this time, my hand collides with the tabletop—*ouch*. Glancing down, I note that the bowl is gone.

"I'd say I'm sorry. But I'm not." I turn towards the deep, gravelly voice. My face flushes, and I immediately regret my decision. The corner of his mouth lifts in a knowing, crooked smile. And my core clenches with want. I shake the traitorous thoughts away and focus on rekindling my rage.

"I'm hungry," I growl like a feral animal. My hand covers his as I make another fleeting attempt to snatch the bowl back.

"Let me take you out to dinner, then. I rarely recommend it, but even a crappy burger from the dollar menu would be better for you than that garbage."

"Do I even know you?" I ask in all seriousness. I don't think I've had that much to drink yet... but maybe I have? He's certainly ordering me around like he knows me well enough. Then again, I'd like to believe—drunk or not—I wouldn't forget a face as handsome as his. Maybe alcohol is the problem here. My whiskey goggles are what's making him so damn dreamy, and causing the warmth of his hand to send a bolt of electricity straight to my clit.

"No, you don't know me." He reaches up and brushes my hair back. Closing the gap between us, he whispers in my ear, "But I'd like you to."

I cross my legs and squeeze my thighs tightly together. I really hope I'm not as wet as I expect I am. He pulls back, and his blue-green eyes caress the curves of my body. My nipples pebble under his scrutiny. The friction as my chest rubs against the silk of my dress only seems to intensify my unwelcomed arousal. *Oh shit.* I look down and notice the erect mounds standing at attention. I go to tug my jacket shut but end up grasping at air. Turning around, I realize my coat is missing. *Damn it.* The memory of stripping it off and throwing it on the ground comes pouring back. I've always been hotheaded. And let's just say it wasn't my finest moment. I was angry, and I took it out on the jacket. Primarily because he'd recently bought it for me for Christmas, and I wanted nothing more to do with him.

Closing my eyes, I hold back the tears threatening to break the surface, and my cheeks burn. Suddenly, a gentle warmth that smells of cedar and mint surrounds me. I crack a lid, risking a glance, and notice a wide black peacoat draped around my shoulders.

"You looked... cold," he muses, before flashing me a smile that effectively evaporates whatever panties I'm wearing.

"I appreciate the gesture and all. But seriously, I've just had about the worst night of my life, and all I really want to do is drink myself into oblivion and forget pretty faces like yours exist." I shrug off his jacket. He places a large hand on my shoulder and halts me.

"Want to talk about it?" I hate the pity clear in his gaze as he slightly tilts his head to the side.

"I doubt you're as talented a listener as my buddy Jameson here."

His cocky smirk returns. "I'm a quick learner. Perhaps he could teach me a thing or two?" Just as he settles on the stool to my left, a steaming-hot burger is pushed in front of me. I turn to see Sean studying the situation carefully. His muscles flex under his tight, black, long-sleeved *KO's* shirt. Although he never went pro or became a famous fighter like Killian, it had nothing to do with his skillset and everything to do with needing to be here to care for his little sister.

5

"You good, Nita?" Sean asks, cracking his knuckles.

I roll my eyes at the unnecessary display of testosterone. No, Sean isn't jealous or claiming his territory. We all grew up in the same neighborhood, playing on the streets from sunup to sundown. I didn't have any big brothers, or a dad—or anyone really—to help intimidate boys and kick their asses if they did me wrong. Sean and Killian didn't hesitate to fill that role. It's strictly platonic. Grasping the giant burger with both hands, I lift it towards my mouth. "I am now." A moan slips from my lips as the savory flavors hit my tongue. Out of the corner of my eye, I don't miss the way the mystery man adjusts himself. Seeing I'm not the only one affected by our exchange gives me a boost of confidence. Closing my eyes, I take a huge bite and put on a spectacle of enjoyment while moaning loud enough to draw the attention of nearby onlookers. I set down the food and wipe my fingers with a napkin. "That is the best thing I've ever had in my mouth."

Sean chuckles, shaking his head. "Need anything else?" I don't miss how he glances at my new self-imposed babysitter, showing that "anything" includes kicking the guy out if need be.

"No, I don't need anything else." The man's tense shoulders ease at my words. "But my friend here could use a glass and a burger of his own."

"Sure thing." Sean snickers, turning on his heel and walking away.

"So." Mr. Momma-didn't-teach-me-any-manners reaches over and snatches a fry from my plate. He dunks it in the house-special dipping sauce before stalling, with the crispy potato just outside his pillowy lips. Lips that I desperately want to press mine against to discover if they are as soft as I assume they are. Then he looks at me. "You think I'm pretty." My brow furrows in annoyance. Of course, out of everything I said earlier, all he heard was that I found him attractive. I snatch the fry from between the pads of his large fingers and shove it into my mouth.

"Look, if you are going to intrude on my evening of drinking and wallowing in self-pity, I am laying a few ground rules."

"I've never been the best at following rules," he states, extending a hand and rubbing circles on my inner wrist. His focus is like a hawk as he monitors my pounding pulse. Everything, including his hands, is muscular and well defined. Visions of him bending me over his lap and giving me a spanking cause my body to shiver. *I've been such a bad girl.* I snatch my arm away and hold it to my chest. *We hate men right now, remember?*

"Rule number one: I am not going to fuck you." His brow raises in challenge. As though cautioning: *If that's what you need to tell yourself, sweetheart. But you're not fooling anyone.* "You wanna sure thing? I suggest scooting over three stools. No doubt Shelly will lend a hand... or a mouth... or whatever it is you're looking for."

He turns and glances at the blonde, whose

dress appears as though it is painted on. With a shrug, he looks back at me. "Not interested." *Okay, maybe his taste isn't all that bad... but I still don't trust him.*

"Number two: don't touch my food." He stops midair, his hand hovering above my plate. "I am angry and liable to bite your finger off."

Ignoring my warning, he picks up the fry and slowly pushes it into his mouth. The act is annoyingly sensual. Fuck, if him eating a deep-fried potato is making me this hot and bothered, I am doomed. "Okay, and what else?"

"Huh?" I can't quite remember what we were discussing, as I sit mesmerized by the powerful muscles in his jaw flexing while he chews.

A rough, calloused finger lifts my chin, forcing my gaze to meet the hypnotic swirl of his blue-green eyes. "You said you had a few rules. Where I come from, that means at least three. So far, you've only given me two."

Oh yeah, my rules. What was the third one again? Did I even have three? I lift my shoulder in a shrug. "If you break it, I'll let you know."

Anita

CHAPTER TWO

"So, let me get this straight..." Declan (my mystery man) grabs a nearby napkin to wipe away the bit of juice dripping from the corner of his mouth. Just in time. Because I was about to make an ass of myself and clean it up with my tongue. To distract my mind from my sordid thoughts, I take a swig of the beer Sean offered me instead of my favorite whiskey—it's better than being cut off altogether. "The entire night was his plan?" I nod. "You meet him at the restaurant, which—no offense—should have been a huge red flag. Because no way in fuck would I let my girl cab it to our date. Especially not dressed like that." He gestures his inked hand to the length of my body that's clad in a tight, low-scoop dress with lacey long sleeves. Although all the important bits are covered, it leaves little to the imagination. "Sorry, back to the point. When you get there, outside the fucking restaurant, he ends it."

I mumble my agreement while taking another swig. It sounds worse, hearing it relayed back to me. How could I allow myself to be so blindsided? *Again.* I'd like to think of myself as a sensible woman. But clearly, there is a kink in my armor.

"Fuck," he grumbles to himself, along with something about kicking my ex's ass.

"It'll be taken care of," Sean chimes in before I get to protest. I roll my eyes, as some form of manly telepathic alliance occurs between them. "Don't give me that look, Nita. He knows the rules."

"Rules?" Declan looks between us. "You seem to enjoy those around these parts."

I wave my hand, signaling Sean to shut up. "It's nothing but schoolyard BS that we're all way too old for." I narrow my gaze at the overtalkative bartender. While I appreciate him having my back, I am a grown-ass woman. Sure, Steve ended up being another in a long line of jerks. However, he doesn't deserve to spend the next several months eating through a tube. Sean refills my drink before having another silent exchange with Declan and walking off.

"Not that I'm afraid of a little friendly competition, but is there something going on there?"

I raise my eyebrow at his question.

"Competition?" I muse. "I already told you I'm not going to fuck you."

His eyes darken, a storm brewing behind the glare. My skin tingles as he walks his fingertips up my forearm to my bicep. "And I already told *you*... I'm not a fan of obeying the rules." A knowing smirk pulls at his lips as my skin pebbles with his admission. "Besides, there is a lot more to compete for than sex."

"Like what?" I huff, hardly above a whisper.

He leans in closer, the single word hot on my ear. "You."

I suck in a sharp breath as he pulls back. "I need to pee," I say abruptly, standing on my wobbly heels. He reaches out to help me balance. I turn both of my palms to him, the universal sign for: *Not so fast, pal.* "I've got it." Navigating the crowded bar and only bumping into a few other patrons, I make it to the bathroom stall and lock the door behind me. Placing my hand to my chest, I rest against the entryway, willing my pulse to slow down. "What's wrong with me?" I ask myself. "*I need to pee.* Who says that to a guy as hot as he is? Oh yeah! Me, that's who," I groan. But it isn't just my excited utterances that have me caught off guard. Hardly five hours ago, I got dumped by my boyfriend in front of the restaurant that was supposed to host our Valentine's date. A setup, mind you, which was one hundred percent his idea. I never bought into all the hearts and roses propaganda. When he suggested going out, I said we should just eat dinner at the pub and play darts (like we do most weekends). The big hair, the cocktail dress, and the too-high heels are not me. *But Steve liked it.* Ugh, add that to my laundry list of overlooked red flags. I've known him since middle school. We never ran in the same circles; he was the football jock, and I was anything but a cheerleader. I figured we were in our thirties and those high school labels no longer mattered.

After releasing my aching bladder, I shuffle to the sink, finally taking the risk and looking at my reflection in the mirror. It isn't as horrendous as I thought. My eyes are red and glassy. The black liner is a little smudged; fortunately, it looks like I am trying to relive my early 2000s punk-rock days. While I don't outwardly exhibit the hot mess I really am internally, I still hate the girl in the mirror. She isn't me. This was me allowing Steve to mold me into the girlfriend he wanted. And this was me being too stupid to realize it. The worst part of it all is that, in the end, I still wasn't good enough. I'm not angry that we broke up, but I *am* upset with myself that it was him doing the dumping—which makes me wonder how long I would have let his control continue. Would I have woken up in five years as the picture-perfect Stepford wife? An idealistic monstrosity my ex created? A culmination of the "best" female attributes, hand-selected by Dr. Frankenstein himself? And the complete opposite of everything I thought myself to be...

My chest clenches as I think of Declan sitting out there. He didn't approach and flirt with the real me. No, I'm still in costume for a role

12

I no longer want to play. I have no doubt he's just another Steve waiting to happen. I'd rather die old and alone, surrounded by cats, than let myself fall into the same routine of pretending to be someone I'm not. Yes, tomorrow I am going to the shelter and getting my first of many furry feline friends, to keep from making one grave mistake too many.

Reaching into my purse, I pull out my emergency scrunchy and tug my hair up into a messy bun. I can't do anything about the cosmetic face paint at the moment. I am going to need a commercial-grade cleaner to get this shit off. Tonight, when I get home, I am burning this dress, the shoes, and every other piece of Steve that exists at my place. My mind made up, I straighten my spine and stroll back to the bar.

My steps—and overall resolve—falter briefly as I observe Declan leaning over the bar, his short dark hair sticking up in all directions as though he just ran his hand through it. The sleeves of his navy-blue shirt are haphazardly rolled, displaying the thick black ink that crawls from his fingers up and under his sleeves. *I wonder how far they go?* "No, bad Nita," I chastise myself. *Remember, this man is the epitome of tomorrow's sober regrets. And even if he wasn't, you have to wait at least the customary grace period of two weeks before jumping on a new dick.* Fuck, maybe I need to do a thirty-day cleanse. Get the taste of douchebag out of my system. And hope that, when I'm finally ready to take in solids again—literally, *take in*, like the *solid* object the man in front of me is sporting between his thighs—I'll have developed a more sophisticated taste palate. Puffing out my chest, I approach my spot at the bar, but I don't bother reclaiming my seat.

"I was worried you might have fallen in." I avoid looking directly at his charming smile as well as the pools in his eyes—the unique combination of blue and green reminds me of the hot springs I visited in Yellowstone. Nope, I don't even peek up. Because if I do, my determination will crack. "Anita, is something wrong? Did someone hurt you?" He stands and possessively grabs my arm, shielding me as he seeks out a nonexistent perpetrator.

I squeeze my eyes shut as I peel his grip from my wrist. Removing his touch hurts like ripping duct tape from my flesh. I hate how much I miss his hands on me. "No, nothing happened. Just... look, I need to go home. I appreciate you hanging out and listening to me bitch. But this was a bad idea." I see Sean approach and wave him down. "Can I settle my tab later?"

"No worries, I know you're good for it." He glances between Declan and me, using his *super-human bartender senses* to discern the sudden shift in atmosphere. "You need me to take you home?"

I hold up my phone. "No, I got an Uber coming. I appreciate the offer." Although I live within walking distance, I will not risk journeying home in the dark and cold of winter, drunk and dressed like... *this*. Crime isn't too bad in our little bubble, within the west end of St. Paul, but awful shit can happen anywhere.

"Fine, just text me when you get home. You know I hate that Uber shit." Sean leans down, disappearing behind the bar, and pops up a second later with a sweatshirt that he tosses at me. "Put this on. It's cold."

Laughing, I pull the oversized hoodie over my head. It sits as long as my dress, at my mid-thigh. "You got it. Night, Sean." I turn to Declan; his mouth opens as if he's ready to say something. "Goodbye, Declan." Not giving him a chance to reply, I tug my purse strap up, turn on my heel, and walk out into the freezing night air. Thank God I have a high tolerance for this weather—a natural adaptation from having lived in Minnesota my whole life. Nevertheless, bare legs and negative-ten-degree temperatures aren't a brilliant combination. My back is blasted with warm air as the front door of the bar swings open. I don't bother turning around to see who's there. We may have just met, but I recognize the woodsy scent of his cologne immediately. "Go back inside."

He stands next to me, pulling out and lighting a cigarette, before tucking his hands in his pockets. He talks with the rolled tobacco skillfully resting against his bottom lip. "If you think I'm going to let you stand out here alone, clearly you got a poor impression of me that needs rectifying."

The large exhale I release manifests as an immediately visible cloud of cold air. I turn to face him, and damn, I wish I didn't. Sporting a dark beanie with the collar of his coat turned up, he's the true-to-life embodiment of a leading man, the image sending my ovaries into overdrive. "There is nothing to rectify. I told you I'm not—"

"Yeah, I heard you the first couple of times. *You're not going to fuck me.*" In a huff of annoyance, he takes a long drag before tossing the cigarette to the ground. "Seriously, who made you think that's all you are worth?" Whatever argument I had dies on my lips. I was prepared to counter every excuse. But I wasn't expecting... *that.* "Don't get me wrong..." His sexy smirk reappears. "I am eager and so very willing to hear you scream my name as I pound into that sweet pussy of yours. But who convinced you that you were good for nothing more than a decent fuck? I'd appreciate the list of each one of those assholes, so I can teach them how to treat a woman."

I hug myself, in an attempt to deflect his— while roughly delivered—intrinsically kind words. "Look, I already got two guys in there threatening to kick all my boyfriends' asses. I don't need another."

With a growl, he grabs my hip, pulling me closer. At this angle, I have to crane my neck to see his face. "Well, they are doing a piss-poor job, then."

"You don't even know me," I gasp as I feel something long and hard rub against my stomach. My conviction is quickly diminishing as I loop my arms over his shoulders and play with the short hairs at his nape.

"What do you think I've been trying to do all night?" As though I've been possessed, I lick my lips and lean up on my tippytoes, his mouth looking more appetizing by the minute. My skin is dying to know if that stubble will burn as amazingly as I imagine it will. His large hand snakes around my hip to squeeze my ass cheek firmly. *Yeah, he's definitely a spanker.* "What about your rules?" His tone sounds as desperate as I feel.

"What rules?" While part of me is feigning ignorance, the whiskey and beer have made the earlier proclaimed restrictions hazy. Or at least not as relevant at the moment. My core clenches as he leans down to close the distance between us. Shutting my eyes, I prepare to throw caution to the wind and embrace the *now*. After a year of adequate, albeit vanilla sex, I deserve to have my world rocked. *Even if it is just for tonight.* The rapid beat of my pulse pounding in my ears drowns out the late-night city traffic. In the darkness, everything is spinning. And that's when I realize that *clench* is more of a burn, traveling up from my gut and through my esophagus. *Oh shit!*

Anita

CHAPTER THREE

"**D**id someone beat me over the head last night?" I grumble to no one in particular. The words slice my throat like razor blades. And sunlight burns my retina as I crack one of my lids open and immediately shut it. Although it'll probably cost me my sight, at least the brief glimpse of my surroundings confirms I'm home. The problem is I don't exactly remember how I got here. I have a hazy memory of being dumped by Steve, then drinking away my sorrows at KO's. A smile stretches across my face as I recall my chance encounter with the handsome stranger. A smile that is immediately replaced by a frown, as the recollection of blowing him off and storming out of the bar resurfaces. After that though? Nothing...

Despite the fact my muscles and head are yelling

at me to lie back down, I ignore them and force myself to get up. Shuffling my feet and tripping on some strewn about clothing, I make my way to the window and close the curtains, granting myself the ability to open my eyes. Without really looking and based on habit, I journey to my bathroom. As I prepare to wash up in the mirror, I am shocked. And not just because I am wearing my *'04 Vans Warped Tour* t-shirt. Oh, no, there is so much more to it. I am dumbstruck as I take in my clean face and partially damp hair, and realize I must have showered last night before passing out—which, if I drank as abundantly as I think I did, never would have happened. It wouldn't have been possible. Maybe the change of clothes, because that dress and thong were uncomfortable, and I would have rather slept naked than painfully confined by the skin-tight material. But on a good day, I forget to wash my face before bed. *I better text Sean and thank him.* Between my two childhood friends, he's the only one who would have taken the time to clean me up. Killian would have thrown me on my bed with a bucket, some aspirin, and a glass of water, then wished me luck before bidding me farewell. Great guy, but definitely not a caretaker.

Me: Thanks for last night.

I quickly comb out the mess of tangled curls from sleeping with my head wet, then throw my hair up into a lazy bun.

Me: Next time, though, skip the shower. I almost broke my brush trying to tame this mane.

20

It'll probably take another shower and properly washing and drying to fix this fiasco. But right now, my growling stomach is more demanding than the bird's nest I'm sporting. My phone vibrates on the counter, but I don't look at the message, knowing it's probably some jackass remark from Sean. One that'll require at least a couple of cups of coffee in my system to read. I stall, with my hand on the knob of the bathroom door, as I hear the clinking of metal pans resonating from my kitchen. *Did Tiffany come home last night?* No, she usually stays at Joel's place. In all honesty, it's like she hardly lives here anymore. I roll my eyes. *Unless Sean messaged her about my breakup...* As my best friend, she'd stop mid-orgasm to hurry home and comfort me.

"You didn't need to rush to my rescue, ya know," I holler as I exit the bathroom and make my way to the kitchen. Although I hate the thought of her leaving Joel to be here with me now, I am equally grateful for the delicious scent filling the small space. "But the bacon is much appreciated. Tell Joel I—" I stop mid-step. And not at the sight of my bubbly blonde roommate. Not unless she morphed into a tall man with dark disheveled hair, who appears almost as hungover as I am. Instinctively, I grab between my thighs, checking for any sign of the sex I have zero recollection of instigating.

"If I fucked you, you'd know," he says, a hint of laughter in his voice as he dishes up food.

"How... why are you here?" I left him last night.

21

Oh my god, is he stalking me? I take a cautious step back and immediately groan as I remember I left my phone in the bathroom. I glance to the side. The room is close enough... I should be able to make it there and call 9-1-1, before he can break the door down. I take off running but barely make it a step as two enormous arms wrap around my waist. Despite the hangover from hell, I quickly recall the self-defense training Killian gave me. Taking a step forward to balance myself, I use my elbow and swing back, aiming for my attacker's jaw. We both holler out in pain as the blow connects. It may hurt like fuck, but at least he let me go. Not wasting another second, I rush to the bathroom, engage the lock, and collapse to the floor. I hold a palm over my chest and attempt to steady my breathing. A squeal leaves my throat as the door rattles behind me.

"Anita, open up!" He pounds again.

"I'm calling the police," I reply as I rush to grab my phone. My hands are shaking, and I keep messing up my unlock code. "Fuck."

"Anita, please open the door." He sighs. "I didn't mean to scare you. I brought you home last night and didn't want to leave you alone."

"Nice try. I left you at the bar, stalker!"

He releases a muffled string of expletives. "Yes, and I followed you outside."

"See! *Stalker.*"

"Damn it, Anita... I need you to think *real* hard, sweetheart. After how much you drank last night,

I am surprised by your agility this morning—obviously I'm off my game. But, for the love of Christ, please... *please* try to remember." His heavy footsteps echo as he walks away from the bathroom.

The repetitive chime of incoming messages stops me from opening my keypad.

Sean: Anytime.

Sean: Wait!

Sean: What are you talking about?

Sean: Are you okay?

Sean: Answer me.

Sean: You've got two minutes before I come over.

I draw a sharp breath. *Think, Nita. While you seem to have terrible taste in guys, you generally have better radar than this.* I remember Sean giving me his hoodie, then walking outside and waiting for my Uber. That's right. Declan came out and lit a smoke. We talked. Exchanged snarky comments. He had his hands on me. I was ready to kiss him. And then... *Oh. My. God!* The vibration in my hands pulls me out of my mini meltdown.

Sean: I'm on my way.

My thumbs move faster than they ever have before.

Me: I'm fine. Sorry. False alarm.

Sean: Proof of life.

I shake my head before taking the requested picture. I flip him the bird, and the camera flashes.

Not a smart move. If I wasn't blind before, I sure am now.

Sean: Cute. This one will be posted on the wall of shame.

I tell him off—but only in my head—as I rise from the linoleum and rush to the sink to make myself a little more presentable. I brush my teeth again and apply some tinted moisturizer and lip balm. Better, although he'll probably still think I'm psycho. I make my way back out and see Declan eating breakfast at the small table in the kitchen. Hesitantly, I take a seat in the adjacent chair, where he set another plate of food and orange juice. *For me.* A flush creeps up my neck as I notice the large red welt on his jaw. It'll definitely leave a bruise.

"I'm sorry about that," I mumble as I take a bite of the perfectly crisped bacon.

He gives me a half smile. "Don't be. It was a good shot."

"Still, I can't believe I..."

"Threw up all over me right before I was going to kiss you." I cast my eyes down in shame. I've never thrown up from drinking before. *Like, ever.* The timing couldn't have been worse. It definitely wasn't a first I was looking to share. Especially with the gorgeous man in front of me. *Well, it's been a good run. I guess I'll go bury myself in a hole now.* "I know you said you didn't want to fuck me. But I assumed that was you playing hard to get, and not out of pure repulsion over the thought."

"Oh my god, no." I cover my face with my hands. "It wasn't that. I mean, I wanted…"

His rough fingers tug my wrists down, and he cups my chin, forcing me to look at him. "I know." He brushes a loose strand of my hair back and tucks it behind my ear.

"Still… thank you. You didn't have to…" His growl causes my vocal cords to clam up.

"You really need to make me that list, sweetheart."

"Who are you?" I search deep within those hazel depths, as if they hold the answers to every one of my prayers. That fluttering in my chest picks up again as my body warms and tingles in that special way. I must still be drunk. *And delusional.* Because there is no way this man is actually real.

"I can assure you… I'm definitely the real deal." *Oh shit, did I just say that out loud?* "And I haven't shown you anything yet."

Declan

CHAPTER FOUR

The past twenty-four hours have been—fuck, I can't even describe how they've been. Killian reached out to me last year, after the news broke about me tearing my ACL. We met on the circuit a few times before he was forced to retire. I thought maybe talking to him would give me some clarity, help me make my decision. But when I walked into KO Murphy's—the pub that shares both Killian's name and his love for Irish booze—it was like a jab to the chest. The sight of her sitting there knocked me flat on my ass. I've seen my fair share of scantily clad women during my career, but none as breathtakingly beautiful as this girl. Like a moth to the flame, I was set on a collision course. For the first time in months, I felt like I was finally where I was supposed to be.

The scent of exotic flowers fills the air as

Anita walks back out into the living room. After breakfast, she took another shower to get her hair *under control*, according to her. Personally, I loved her wild curls sticking every which way. Visions of those soft tendrils fanned across her grey sheets, as she cried out my name, had my dick hard all morning. Granted, I've been sporting a chubby since the moment I laid eyes on her.

"Umm." Self-consciously, she plays with the hem of her worn t-shirt. "I'm not exactly sure what the protocol is right now."

She thinks I'm joking about that list. Last night, as she sat there and told me all about that dipshit ex of hers, in painstaking detail, I witnessed this wildfire burning inside her. Although many outside forces seemed determined to extinguish it, the flames still simmered. Some proper stocking, and that blaze will be roaring to life again.

"Sit," I command, and she obeys. Taking a seat at the farthest end of the couch, she pulls her knees to her chest and hugs them. Her black painted toes peek out from under the frayed bottoms of her too-long-and-too-baggy jeans. "Talk to me."

"I don't know how to do that." *Jab.*

"You had no problem saying what was on your mind last night."

"That was different. Not to mention, it was before... you know." *Jab.*

"I've had worse projectiles thrown my way— believe me. Granted, none of them came from someone as gorgeous as you." The image of

28

her sitting here, in her worn denim and an old band t-shirt, puts last night's entire ensemble to shame. Her displeasure in wearing a minidress and heels was clear, evidenced by the way she frequently adjusted herself and tugged at the hem. Now though, despite her embarrassment, she is at least comfortable in her own skin.

She sighs. "You don't even know me. That girl last night wasn't me." *Hook.*

If her words didn't land like an elbow to the head, the tear rolling down her cheek made for a direct blow.

I'm across the couch in an instant. Grabbing her face in both hands, I use my thumb to wipe away the moisture. "I think that girl last night was more you than you've allowed yourself to be in a long time."

"I rarely dress up like that. My ex, he liked it." Her voice is soft. *Shaky.*

"You could have been wearing a burlap sack, and I still would have thought you were the sexiest thing I've ever seen. I won't lie. That tight little number was hot as fuck. But that wasn't what kept me drawn to you."

"W-what did, then?"

"You. Just you. And the passion with which you spoke, as you explained—in explicit detail—how you planned on detaching your ex's balls."

"After hearing that, you risked bringing me home and disrobing me in the shower?" She raises a brow, revealing a hint of that confident smirk

29

she had at the bar.

"As you may, or I guess *may not* recall, I was a perfect gentleman. Which wasn't easy, by the way. Not with you frequently trying to stick your hand down my pants." I love making her blush.

"I did not."

"Oh, but you did, sweetheart. You were keen to repay my kindness and make up for ruining my shirt. But as I explained to you last night, there is something else I want from you."

"What's that?" Her eyes focusing in on my mouth doesn't go unnoticed. Especially when she darts out her pink tongue to moisten her lips. It would be so easy to lean down and claim her, just as I was going to do last night. While I am eager to show her she's mine, I'm also aware she needs something more from me. Something first.

I bend forward; her lips tickle my own. "A date."

"A date?" she whispers.

"Yes. As I mentioned before, it seems you got the wrong impression of me. And I want to fix that." *Fuck it.* Her mouth opens and I take the opportunity, slamming mine onto hers. It wasn't my original plan. But after her previously offered kiss was interrupted by the sudden reappearance of her partially digested dinner—personally, I blame those fucking candy hearts; those things are nothing but chalky garbage—followed by the torture of having her naked and horny while I scrubbed her down... Well, let's just say my balls helped sway my need for a little self-gratification.

30

Not even after relieving myself in the shower, *twice*, having already tucked her into bed, eased my unrelenting desire.

As her tongue caresses mine, and my scalp burns from her fingers tightly wrapping themselves in my hair, I can see why my manual efforts failed. *My imagination sucks.* Because with this kiss alone, I am seconds away from blowing my load like a preteen who just saw his first titty. I'd be embarrassed if I weren't so desperate for more. Unfortunately, it's the kind of *more* I can't have. Not just yet.

A moan slips from her as I take a small bite of her lip. Reluctantly, I break the embrace and rest my forehead on hers. Our labored breaths create this erotic heat between us.

"Why'd you stop?" She manages between mouthfuls of air.

The muscles in my neck and jaw flex as I restrain myself. Fortunately, years of training have conditioned me to have a punishing level of self-control. Granted, she is testing each one of those nerves as her fingers travel from my head to my back, where she lightly traces a nonsensical pattern. The featherlight touch sends a shiver up my spine. "Date first," is all I can manage to say.

A mischievous grin turns up her lips. "We could count last night as a date."

"Do you really want to be telling our grandchildren one day that our first date ended with you vomiting on me?" *Where the fuck did that come from?* As her hand stills, it's clear she's wondering the same damn thing.

"Grandchildren?" She raises an eyebrow.

"Bushel of 'em," I confirm, barely recognizing the person speaking right now. Not only have I never said anything like this before, I've never even considered it. And the most frightening part is that I mean it. All of it. The few hours of sleep I got last night were filled with dreams of our future. Her belly large and round with children. Corny Christmas photos, where we all wear matching ugly sweaters. White picket fences and Sunday barbecues. In the past, any one of those visions would have been enough to make my balls shrivel up and recede into my body, until we both found a no-strings-attached safe haven.

"Okay..." The uncertainty in her tone squeezes my heart. I can only hope it is because this is all ridiculously fast and confusing. And not because she doesn't feel the same way.

I press one last kiss to her lips, pulling away before either of us can deepen it. "I have some business I need to tend to." Based on the flurry of messages from Killian, it seems we have a lot more to discuss than I originally planned.

"Oh, I understand." She sits straighter and frees herself from my cage-like embrace. "I'm sorry to have kept—"

She stops speaking as a growl emits from my chest. "Tonight?"

"Tonight?"

"Date. You and me, tonight. Anywhere you want to go. I'll pick you up at seven?"

"Okay... wait—no."

"No?" That tightening in my chest has morphed into a full-on vise grip.

"I have to work." A relieved breath escapes my lungs. "I switched shifts to have off last night... for well, you know. Actually, I should get going soon."

"Just tell me when, and I'll be here." Fuck, I hate how desperate I sound. But then again, that is exactly what I am. *Desperate.*

"Well..." She ponders intently and frowns. "Friday?"

"Today is Friday," I state, a bit confused. Is she still drunk?

"Yeah, it was my turn to have Friday, Saturday, and Sunday off. But I traded for... Never mind, it doesn't matter... Anyway, we work three on and three off. Except, with the rotation swap, I am stuck doing my shifts back-to-back—crappy downside to schedule changes. Thursday is technically free, but I'll need to catch up on sleep just to function. Sorry... that was probably more information than you needed..."

"Shit." I rub my palm over my face, thinking about how insane that sort of schedule must be. "What do you do for work?"

A smile tugs at her lips. "I'm a nurse."

Of course she is. I groan as images of her in

a naughty nurse's uniform come to mind. "I can wait." Her grin widens, and her bare face glows. There's no need for her to be painted up like last night; she's breathtaking all her own. In that moment, I decide that, no matter what, I'll make sure she smiles like that every day for the rest of our lives. I rub my nose against her cheek before whispering in her ear, "I've been waiting for you my whole life. One more week is nothing in the grand scheme of things. But, Anita." Her breath hitches. "You're mine, and on Friday, I plan on showing you exactly what that means."

Declan

CHAPTER FIVE

Entering the small gym, I close my eyes and inhale. The stench of body odor fills my lungs and burns my nostrils as it's sucked down. The grunts and thuds, the sound of gloves to bags, and the slap of fists to flesh are like a lullaby. I don't think I'll ever stop loving this. My shoulders slump. *And that's part of the problem.* It doesn't take me long to find Killian. What surprises me is finding him in the ring, sporting sparring gear.

"You're late," he mumbles through his mouth guard, which he then removes. "Get suited up and your ass in the ring. We have some shit to discuss."

I give him a crooked smile as I throw my duffle bag on the ground. "I thought you retired?"

He releases a loud belly laugh. "I might have left

the spotlight. But my dumb arse ain't ever leaving the ring. Now quit your gawking and show me what you got." Repositioning his mouth guard, he throws a couple jabs in the air as he warms up.

In a matter of minutes, I'm in my gear and ready to go. I bump fists with Killian, and the dance begins as we shuffle in a circle.

"Nita?" he grumbles as he throws a jab I can easily avoid. With a nod, I offer him a big smile and toss a punch of my own. He sidesteps and spits out his guard. "No face shots?" I do the same and discard the plastic. "I fucking hate those things," he complains. "You break her heart; I'll break your leg." He raises his scarred brow. "The good one." He takes a swipe at my bad ankle, but I see it coming and deflect.

"Yeah, what about her douchebag ex?" I land a small strike to his gut.

He lets out a huff of air. "He'll be dealt with."

"The others?"

His lips curl into a vicious smile. "They got what was coming to them."

"If you care so much about her, then how come you keep letting her date losers? The kind making her question her self-worth?" My question lands hard, just like my next blow.

The atmosphere shifts as Killian's gaze narrows in on me. Clearly, I have struck a nerve. "Do you even know Nita?" I see a spark of white as my ribs burn—a result of the jab he just secured. Before I can react, my foot is swiped out from under me, and I'm staring at the gym ceiling. Killian stands over my prone form, looking just as fierce as he did in his prime. "That's right. You don't. Seeing as you just met her last night." He squats down to my level. My head spins a bit as I gaze up at him. "Let me share some wisdom with you. Nita does what she wants. There ain't no talking her out of something when her mind is made up. And the quickest way to send her running is to tell her what to do."

"If that's true, then why has she been living like a shell of herself, to please her dipshit boyfriend?"

Killian stands tall and rubs a hand over his face, before extending it down to help me off the mat. "I'll kill you if you ever tell her this." The sparkle in his eye verifies he isn't joking. "Nita is the strongest and sometimes dumbest person I know." I raise my fist, prepared to strike, regardless of his injury and lack of proper PPE. "She's had a rough life, and it's led her to make some bad choices. That being said, I love that girl like my own sister. I might not be able to prevent her from dating jackasses. But I will always be in her corner, ready to fight."

I halt. "What kind of life?"

His expression softens as he shakes his head. "That's her place to explain, not mine. You dig?" I nod and run my fingers through my sweat-soaked hair. With a pat on my back, Killian leads me out of the ring and collapses on the bench, where he takes a swig from a bottle before dumping water over himself. "Fucking women," he grumbles, discharging a string of what I assume are Irish expletives. I laugh, thinking about the first time I met him. I'd seen him on stage, his swagger going full steam ahead. Then, later that night— at an after party—we started chatting. And I was surprised when his accent and demeanor completely changed.

"Yeah, your girl giving you problems?" I muse. Based on the number of women he was flirting with last night, I didn't think he was seeing anyone in particular.

"You don't need to be fucking them for them to be a headache." He lets out a heavy breath. "Between Nita and Cassie, I am going to fucking go gray."

"Your sister got boy troubles?" The colorful sentiments he offers under his breath confirm my suspicion. "Need help kicking some ass?" I met Cassie a couple of times when she attended the fights. She's seemed like the type to attract trouble wherever she went. Fortunately, I found out quickly she was his sister. I don't have many rock-solid limits, but other fighters' kin? Yeah, that's a hard no. I never wanted more than a night. And with as much testosterone as these guys have swinging around, a single hot night with someone's sister (or any close relative) would have created drama not worth the fuck. Not when there are plenty of ring bunnies hopping around and looking for a ride, no questions asked.

"Nah, it'll be taken care of." He sighs. "She's moving. It's hard enough looking out for her here. How the fuck am I supposed to keep an eye on her when she lives almost two hours away?"

I shrug. "Sometimes getting away is the right call. You find what you didn't even know you were looking for."

"We're not talking about my sister anymore, are we?" I laugh as he bumps my shoulder. "I guess we should get down to business, then. I'm assuming you came here for a reason other than a chance encounter at my bar."

"How'd you do it?" My pulse quickens as the fear of the unknown takes over.

"I didn't have much of a choice." He looks off into the distance, deep in thought. "I get it, though. Before the accident, a life out of the ring... away from the crowds and spotlight... It wasn't a path I could imagine. Or at least not one I was interested in trying. But shit happens. You grow older. Your priorities change, and you realize there is more to life than the octagon."

I think about his words. He's right. Before the bad hit that tore my ACL, I figured I'd be one of those geriatric fighters, still throwing punches and selling out Pay-Per-Views. I'd die young and a legend. But after the surgery and intensive physical therapy, I no longer feel the same. I hesitate. I'm afraid of the next blow and what type of damage it might cause. When I try to think of life outside the ring, I can't picture it. That was until last night. Unlike Killian, I don't have a family welcoming me home with open arms. I have no one. My friends are fellow fighters, all of whom will slowly fade away when the lights go down. But then, within that darkness, I found a shiny beacon, one brighter than I've ever seen before.

"Based on the dopey-ass grin on your face, I assume you got the answer you were looking for."

Anita

CHAPTER SIX

Glancing down at my phone, I smile. The week is going by painfully slow. It's only Monday, and the thought of having to wait three more days to see Declan is killing me. Perhaps we *could* meet Thursday. Is sleep necessary? Yes, it is. The first time I met him, I was extremely intoxicated. After six twelve-hour shifts, I wouldn't be much better. It's just... I'm dying to be near him again, which is insane, since I have spent all of what? Twelve hours with him? Mostly consisting of me drunk and complaining. Somehow, those few hours have been more meaningful than the countless months or even years I've spent with my previous boyfriends. The only thing getting me through the day is his texts. Some are funny; most are sexy. Especially a few mouth-watering selfies that left me wet and aching for more. Like the image of him in thin gray joggers that showed me exactly what I was missing out on. As much as I enjoyed them, I told him sending those to me while I was working was cruel and unusual punishment. His reply: *I thought you could use a visual while you were alone and thinking of me.* He has no idea.

The problem is, at night, I am not actually alone. I work a twelve-hour shift, five in the evening until five in the morning. By the time I get home, the only thing I am thinking about is my bed. Not in the sexy way he is imagining. After spending the night in the ER, suturing wounds, draining cysts, helping remove objects inserted in regions they shouldn't be, or dealing with serious trauma that comes in, anything— even pleasurable—requires more energy than I have to spare. Pulling my lip between my teeth, I nibble on it as worry takes over. My job is the root cause of many of my relationship issues: the long hours, the unanswered texts when we get slammed, or simply because I go home and pass out with my phone on silent when I'm not on call. As exhausting and sometimes heartbreaking as it is, I love it. I've never thought of doing anything else. Until now. I wouldn't leave nursing. But I could get a job in a private practice and have more reasonable hours, except then I'd miss the excitement and hustle of the ER. There is always something new or dramatic happening. *Could I really give this all up for him?* I let out a silent scream as I hold my head in my hands. *What is wrong with you, Nita?* I am jumping way too far ahead. We haven't even had a date yet.

"Is Steve being, well..." Tiffany taps her chin. "... Steve?"

My chair scratches across the linoleum as I am up and out of it in two seconds, before leaping across the table to hug my best friend—who I haven't seen or spoken to in weeks. Releasing the tight squeeze I have her in, I step back and push her shoulder. "Bitch."

We both laugh. "I missed you too."

"Whose fault is that?" I quirk my brow at her.

"Oh my gosh, Nita," she says wistfully as she collapses in a chair and shrugs off her large puffy coat.

"So...?" I don't bother finishing my inquiry, as she already knows what I'm about to ask.

Her face turns red as she nods. "He asked me to move in." We both squeal as I give her another big hug. While I am sad to lose my roommate and best friend, more than half of her stuff is already over at his place, and I rarely see her anymore.

"I'm happy for you," I say genuinely.

"There's more." Her face is radiant.

"Did he...?" She nods vigorously as she removes her glove and shows off her giant new engagement ring. "Holy shit." I lean in closer and inspect it as though I know anything about diamonds. *I don't.* All I know is it is big and sparkly. Theoretically, it could be fake. Granted, I'd never care. It isn't about the carat or price tag. It's about the love, which knowing Tiffany, she would be glowing even if he had used a Ring Pop.

"That's not all." My jaw drops as she produces an ultrasound photo. "It's still early, but it's there." She points to a small dot on the image. "I'm sorry I didn't tell you sooner. It's just... I found out on Thursday morning, and I wanted Joel to be the first to know. I was so nervous about how he'd react. We never really talked about babies. I mean, we have only been dating for a few months. I almost died when he stormed away from the table. I started crying, then he dropped to his knee and held out the box. I didn't even let him ask before I screamed yes. I guess when it's meant to be, it's meant to be." I hate the frown pulling at my lips. "Oh, hun. I'm sorry. I'm sure Steve will pull his head out of his butt soon."

"We broke up."

"Seriously? Why didn't you say anything? Here I am, going on about getting married and having a baby. Wait, when did you break up? Weren't you guys doing some fancy dinner at that steakhouse? Honestly, I'd been expecting a text from you about being engaged. When I didn't see it, I assumed much like me you were celebrating."

"He dumped me outside the restaurant."

"He didn't!" She gasps, and I nod. "Was it at least after he bought dinner? You take bad news better with a full belly."

"Nope." I pop the *P.* "I met him outside the restaurant. He smiled, hugged me, and I kissed his cheek. Then he said we should break up. That we were moving too fast, and he wasn't sure we had the same priorities. That he thought we could both use some time to think."

"What the fudge does that mean?"

I shrug my shoulders. "We had been fighting about my long hours. We had a big argument a couple of weeks ago, after he made a comment about how when we have children, I wouldn't be working anymore."

"He didn't."

"He did. Don't get me wrong. If I had a baby, I don't know if I would want to work or not. I probably wouldn't want to have the hours I do now. But I was so angry he thought he had a say in that part of my life. That it wasn't a discussion or question, but a demand. The more I think about Steve, the angrier I get. Why was I even with him? I mean, he's hot and all. The sex was satisfying. But besides that, what did I even see in him? All he ever did was want to change me. What's worse is I allowed him to change my clothes, my diet. Fuck, if he would have knocked me up and proposed, I'm sure I would have followed his orders like a good girl. I'm pathetic."

"You're not pathetic, sweetie." She lovingly pats me on the back. "Sometimes we do stupid things for love, or what we mistake as love. For the first couple months of our relationship, I pretended to hate pickles. On our first date, they didn't give Joel a pickle on his sandwich. I don't know why, but I handed him mine and said I didn't like them anyway. It was only a few weeks ago, when I almost went ravenous as he tried to snatch one off my plate, that I revealed the truth. I love them! Now that I think about it, that was probably a sign right there that I'm pregnant, huh? I am not usually territorial over my food—not like you." My cheeks heat as I recall Declan stealing my fries. "What's that?" She gestures to the expression on my face. "I'm missing something."

"After the incident Thursday night, I went to KO's."

"Oh my gosh," she squeals, "did you finally hook up with Sean? Or Killian? Or both?" She gives me a wink.

"No, and no, and eww." I laugh. "Everything with those two is a hundred percent platonic. If you ever camped out with them after a Fourth of July chili cook off, any sexual thoughts you might have had about either of them would evaporate. Like my nose hair. The odor still haunts me..."

"Gross." She waves a hand in front of her face. "But I agree. That would kill any current or future lady boner for sure. So, what happened at KO's?" She props her head on her bent arm as she leans in, giving me her full attention.

"Well, while drinking away my sorrows—"

"No, hun, celebrating your close call. Remember, Steve was not worthy of you and you escaped before any actual damage could be done."

I nod, accepting her point before continuing. "Okay, well, while I was explaining my night to my old friend, Mr. Jameson, this guy approached me. And I just can't explain it. But the chemistry was immediate. At first, I thought my reaction to him was because I was drunk and horny. Then, the next morning he scared the shit out of me in the apartment. I thought he was an intruder, and I elbowed him in the jaw." I laugh recalling the horrifying event. "After I regained my bearings, I was shocked. In the sobering light of day, hungover and mortified by everything that happened, I still wanted him as much as I had the night before. I've never felt so strongly about someone. Not like this. Not so quickly... It's crazy, right?"

"Hold up. I'm confused." She raises her hand. "You took him home? Were you so drunk you didn't remember you brought him here?" I explain the rest of the events from that evening. At least everything I can remember, including the embarrassing projectile vomiting. "Okay," she states hesitantly.

"What?"

"I'm your best friend, right?" I nod as my stomach grows heavy with dread. That's code for: *I have bad news, but you can't be angry because you love me.* "While he sounds dreamy—in that dangerous way I know you go all swoony over—you just broke up with Steve. Someone you've known since middle school and, from what you've told me, is a grade-A loser."

"Yeah..." I seem to be missing her point.

She sighs and says a prayer to the heavens. "What do you know about this guy? What does he do for work? Why was he at KO's? Primarily, only us locals hang out there, except for the occasional fan who wants to meet Killian." I open my mouth to reply, then realize—as I go over our night—that with the exception of his name, he never told me a single thing about himself. "This." She circles her finger at my face. "Right here is how you end up in trouble. You fall, headfirst and blindfolded, then pray you stick the landing. You know his name, right?"

My phone is instantly in my hand and pulling up Google. Why didn't I do this earlier? At least stalk his social media or something... *Declan Adams.* A million results pop up. Then I note that several of them read: *Declan "The Devil" Adams.* "No way." I open the profile. And there he is, in all his shirtless, tattooed, sexy, and oh-so-delicious muscular glory. "He's a fighter." Next, I scroll through countless images of him with other fighters, celebrities... and then women. Lots and lots of women. Tall, drop-dead gorgeous women. The kind of women I'm not and don't want to be. I notice that one of the articles references his home. Out east... in New Jersey. "He's just passing through."

"I'm sorry, sweetie." Tiffany rests her head on my shoulder as she gives me a half hug. Each article is like a stab to the chest. It seems I must be a glutton for punishment. Because I can't stop reading, even though every single one breaks my heart. I really am an idiot. I hardly knew the guy. And yet, somehow, when he mentioned telling our grandchildren how we first met, it was like my future flashed before my eyes. Though it was fast, it was right. But now, I've never felt so wrong. A series of messages lights up my screen. Realizing the popup lists Declan's name, I turn my phone to silent and set it down without reading his texts, knowing if I do, he'll likely put me under his spell once again. *No more, Nita. You deserve someone—no, not just someone. You deserve the one. And that isn't Declan "The Devil" Adams.*

i

Declan

CHAPTER SEVEN

Chugging back my beer, I slam the empty glass on the wood countertop and gesture for Sean to get me another. I've read and reread the texts too many times to count. I don't know where it went wrong. She was flirty and fun one moment, then silence the next. At first, when she didn't reply, I assumed it was because of her job or chaotic sleep schedule. After working a long-ass shift like that, the first thing I would want to do is turn my shit on silent and pass out. I kept sending her funny messages and some memes I found. And possibly a naughty picture or two, knowing she'd get them eventually and hoping they'd bring a smile to her face.

Come Wednesday, my fears were confirmed when I received a single text.

Anita: I can't do this. Stop messaging me.

I replied immediately, asking her what was wrong, if something happened. No response. I even risked calling her, praying to hear her sweet voice so I could rectify whatever went wrong. Straight to voicemail. Not just once, or twice. But too many times to admit.

"Still ignoring you?" Sean inquires as he tops me off. "What did you do?"

"I don't know," I answer honestly.

Sean levels me with a stare. "You didn't try anything, did you?"

"No," I growl. "We kissed. A mutually appreciated kiss, mind you. I wanted to take her on a proper date before going any further, which was the plan for tomorrow. I always imagined when I finally got myself a girl—you know, one worth more than a night—I'd probably fuck it up somehow. Especially since I have never been in a relationship before. But how could I screw it up so badly and not realize what I've done wrong?"

Sean lets out a knowing chuckle. "That's relationships for you." He eases off at my frown. "Seriously, man, I have no clue. I've only had a few solid girlfriends, and I doubt they are writing me any letters of recommendation. Killian would have even less insight to provide. What you need is a woman."

"I have a woman." Well, not technically, at the moment. But those are just minor details to work out. Anita Erickson is mine. Now I just need to figure out how to make sure she understands that. Sean looks around the bar, and his eyes settle on the blonde cozying it up with some large red-haired man. "You do suck at this." I point out. "Not that I'm interested. But usually, when you try to hook someone up, you're supposed to aim for a chick who ain't clearly spoken for."

"Shut up, you idiot." He waves a hand at me. "Yo, Tiff!" The blonde looks at him and then her gaze lands on me. Her smile is immediately replaced by a frown. *Fuck, this chick hasn't even met me yet and she already hates me.* "Get your ass over here."

Even from a distance, I can see her eyes roll. She whispers something into the redhead's ear before sauntering over. With her lips tight and thin, she stands in front of us, arms crossed. "No," she states, the disdain evident in her tone.

"Come on, Tiff, help a fella out," Sean pleads. I look from one to the other, clearly missing something crucial.

"No, he's not good enough for her." At that, my ears perk up. Although her name hasn't been mentioned, I know they are talking about my Anita.

"Like fuck I'm not." She gasps at my sudden outburst, but quickly straightens her spine.

"Look, Anita needs more than some one-night stand, looking to pass through town. She deserves a man, a real one. Not just muscles and pretty words. But someone who will be there and support her, who lifts her up. As her best friend, I will not let her fall prey to another loser."

"If you were such a good friend, how'd you let her date that asshole for so long?" She shrinks at the mention of Anita's ex. "Or the ones before?"

The red-haired man is immediately at the blonde's side with a palm on her shoulder. Before he can speak, she raises a finger, indicating she can handle herself. "Touché. I'll admit I have been distracted lately. But not seeing the signs, versus allowing her to knowingly walk into a train wreck, those are two very different things."

"I feel like I am missing something." I rub my forehead to ease the ache.

"What happened, Tiffany?" Sean takes over. "At least spell it out for the poor guy, so he can move on."

"She Googled you." Her smile is one of satisfaction, as if she won some grand prize.

Googled me? "Oh."

"That's right, Declan "The Devil" Adams. She knows *all* about you."

"Dude, you didn't tell her you were a fighter?" Sean shakes his head, mumbling under his breath about how stupid I am.

"No," I admit shamefully. "I didn't think it mattered, considering..."

"Considering what?" Tiffany's smirk drops.

"I came to see Killian, to talk to him about when he retired. I've been weighing my options since my injury." Reaching behind my head, I rub my neck. "But the second I laid eyes on her, I knew I was done."

"You're quitting?" Tiffany and Sean say in unison.

I nod as I contemplate what to do.

"So, you aren't going back to Jersey to live in your mansion, surrounded by gorgeous ring girls?"

"No," I bite. The big man shifts Tiffany behind him. "I haven't quite figured out the living situation yet. My plan was to discuss that with Anita. Tomorrow. During our date." I make it a point to stare at Tiffany. I recognize she's not fully to blame for the misunderstanding between Anita and me; nevertheless, she seems to be getting the brunt of my frustration. "But definitely no ring girls. Or any other girls. Ever again."

"Seriously? You just met her." Her statement is not judgmental; it's more like she's looking for verification.

"When you know, you know." At this, Tiffany's face lights up with a bright smile as she rubs a giant rock on her finger. And the look she's giving me says she knows exactly what I'm talking about.

"Okay, I'll help you," she suddenly declares. "But just this once. If you mess up after this, that's on you."

"Deal," I agree, but only because I know I won't screw it up. At least, not like this first time. There are a lot of unknowns for me right now. However, there is one thing I am certain of: no matter where

I am or what I'm doing, I want—no, I need—Anita in my life.

Anita

CHAPTER EIGHT

Rolling over, I grab my cell from the nightstand. I glance at the time and let out a sigh. It's two thirty. Not that I didn't need the sleep after such a long week... it just feels like I am missing something. As crazy as it sounds, I was looking forward to our date tonight. Although it was my choice to cut him off, I won't lie. A part of me is aching to call him. You know, enjoy whatever time we have together.

You deserve more than that.

I do. I know I do... Except, that one embarrassing night and awkward morning have had a longer-lasting impact on me than any of my previous relationships. Steve and I were dating for almost eight months. And, besides some residual anger over the whole situation, I have paid him little to no mind. When his name popped up on my caller ID—more than likely to coordinate picking up the few belongings I still have at his place and vice versa—I felt no compulsion to speak with him. I don't need any additional closure. Tiffany was right. *He did me a favor.* I pick up the phone again and glance at Declan's name. I worry my lip between my teeth as my thumb hovers dangerously close to the call button. One accidental slip, and the phone will dial out.

Closing my eyes, I prepare to make a mistake that will probably cost me my heart. Because let's face it: if he has me this tied up in knots after a few nice words and a kiss that rocked my world, spending another second with him will be devastating to my emotional fortitude. Despite the guaranteed heartache, a few moments of pure bliss seem worth the tears and ice cream later. Commotion out in the living area has me sitting up and dropping my phone. My shoulders relax as I remember Tiffany mentioned stopping by to bring some more stuff over to Joel's today.

Tossing the blankets to the side, I hop off the bed. In a rush, I slip on a pair of shorts and sneak a sports bra on under my t-shirt. I'm not sure why; it's not like I have a giant rack or anything. But for some reason, the idea of letting these puppies roam free when company is over doesn't sit well with me. In the past, I've thrown on a bra quickly when pizza is being delivered, then stripped it off the second I laid the boxes on the counter.

After getting dressed enough to feel presentable, I rush into the bathroom to clean up.

I spit my toothpaste into the sink and inhale as the smell of bacon fills the air. Excited to be fed, I stow away my toothbrush and walk out to the living room.

"While I appreciate the bacon, you are going to need to do more than that to make up for ditching me," I tease as I enter the archway.

"I'm not going anywhere, sweetheart."

I shriek as Declan steps out from my kitchen with two plates in hand. I brandish my phone as though it were a sword. "Stop." He freezes. "Okay, this has gone too far. Even if you did make me breakfast, this is breaking and entering. You've reached stalker level five."

"I didn't break in." He smiles. "I have a key."

"Did you make a copy while I was sleeping?" I ask in disbelief, as I clutch the phone to my chest. How could I be so wrong about him? That's what I get for thinking someone so deliciously dangerous and charming could also be a good guy. He sets the plates down on the small table before taking cautious steps towards me. "Stop, or I'll call Killian." He continues to get closer. "His brother, Cian, is an Army Ranger. He could kill you and make sure no one ever finds your body." I inch back, aiming to retreat to the bathroom, but run into the wall. By the time I realize my mistake, Declan has me caged between him and the hard surface, his thick, corded arms testing the elasticity of his shirt's fabric and preventing my escape. I close my eyes and try to recall the moves Killian taught me for this situation; however, my assailant's woodsy cologne is scrambling my circuits, causing me to lick my lips and clench my thighs. I'll admit I've had an intruder fantasy before. I just never imagined that, when it happened, I'd actually be turned on. You know, I assumed the reality of it all would make me panic, except right now, my only concern is that if he doesn't make a move soon, I might do something stupid. Like wrap myself around him and beg him to fuck me.

I gasp as his fingertips tickle my skin, bristling the sensitive nerve endings, while he brushes a strand of my hair back. "Tiffany gave me her key."

"She did what?" Opening my eyes, I swallow hard, as I notice how close those turquoise pools are to me.

He nuzzles against my cheek, his scruff burning in all the right ways, and I now find myself desperate to push his head lower to where I really need him. "It appears we've had a small misunderstanding, Anita." A half moan, half cry slips out as he presses his erection into my stomach. He's speaking words. Likely important ones. But at the moment, he might as well be one of the teachers from *Charlie Brown*, because all I hear is: *wah, wah, wah.* "You Googled me." His hand snakes up and under my shirt, and a rough, calloused thumb massages the band of my bra. "I wasn't hiding myself from you." He nibbles my ear. "If I wanted to hide anything, I wouldn't have given you my actual name."

"New Jersey... ring girls." Common sense says I should push him off and form full sentences. But my traitorous body refuses to do so. Instead, she pulls him closer as I hook a leg over his hips. At this angle, his rigid member rubs my clit perfectly through my thin sleep shorts. One more, and I'll come before he even actually touches me. This can't be normal, can it?

He squeezes my ass and presses into me harder. My body shakes as I try to hold on. "No ring girls. Never again," he grits out through clenched teeth. "The rest, I wanted to... discuss... date—fuck."

"Please," I beg. My previous concerns seem miniscule compared to my throbbing core, desperate to be filled by him. Even if it is only this one time...

He grabs my hair, forcing my neck to arch forward. "Oh my god," I pant as he bites down, then licks the wound. The room spins, and suddenly my cheek and palms are flush against the cool plaster wall. Eagerly, he rips my shorts and underwear down in one tug. I finish toeing them off as I hear his pants unbuckle. As though I'm in heat, I arch my back and angle my dripping core towards him, presenting him with an offering. And secretly praying the sacrifice will be worth it in the end. A foil wrapper opens, and a moment later, I feel his large head pressed at my entrance.

"This won't be gentle," he warns. His thumbs trace the globes of my ass.

I glance over my shoulder and give him a half smile. "I didn't ask you to be." With a painful grip, he holds my hips and pushes into me. I scream in pain and pleasure, as if he is tearing me apart and making me whole all at once. Finally fully sheathed, he pauses and allows my muscles a moment to adjust.

"You good?" The strain in his voice tells me he's holding on by a thread.

"I've never been better."

He isn't gentle, as he warned, while he vigorously pounds into me. And like a chant, I scream his name, not caring one bit about the awkward glances I'm going to get from my neighbors later. If they were being fucked like I am right now, they'd understand I couldn't be quiet even if I wanted to. Pulling my head back by my ponytail, he growls in my ear. "You feel that, sweetheart?" I moan my agreement—at least, that's what I think I do. His other hand snakes around and presses against my clit. Black spots fill my vision. "You're mine. I'm not going anywhere."

"I'm yours," I whisper.

"Louder, sweetheart," he demands as he slams his cock to the hilt.

"I'm yours!" I shout at the top of my lungs.

"Fuck right you are." His thumb matches the tempo of his thrusts. "And you know what else, sweetheart? I'm all yours." My throat goes raw as I vocalize my release. The pulse of his orgasm forces mine farther over the edge, and I watch as fireworks burst around me. As I come down, I realize we are seated on the floor. Him, cradling me in his bare lap. Both of us, panting and still breathless.

"Did you mean it?" As I regain consciousness, his words register.

He pulls me closer and rests his chin on my head. "Every fucking word."

Declan

CHAPTER NINE

I can't take my eyes off her. And I don't want to. In awe, I observe her as she swirls her French fry in the sauce. I'm envious when she brings it to her mouth, wishing it were my cock instead—despite the fact that, mere hours ago, she had those same lips around me as we washed up in the shower. It seems now that I've tasted her, I'm addicted, desperate for my next high. When we stepped out from her apartment building, both of our stomachs demanded sustenance—after our marathon of sex. Our "brunch" had long-since grown cold, and only the bacon remained edible, which wasn't nearly enough calories to replace what we burned off. And for the first time since I was fourteen, I didn't feel compelled to light a smoke the moment I walked outside. The only thing I wanted to taste, or inhale, was her.

Although I have my own food, I reach down and steal one of her fries and pop it in my mouth.

"I told you my rule," she scolds playfully. "Don't. Touch. My. Food."

"And I told you how I feel about those rules." I give her a cocky smile. "Besides, as I recall, we broke the first one—several times—prior to coming here. You didn't seem to mind then. If anything, you begged me to... *break it again.*"

"Asshole." She laughs and throws a fry at me. I catch it with my mouth. Anita studies me for a moment before her smile drops to a frown. "What now?"

"What do you mean?" She seriously can't still be questioning this. *Us.*

"What are we?" She pulls her lip between her teeth. Reaching over, I grasp her jaw with my thumb and forefinger. I don't take my eyes off her steely orbs.

"I'm only going to explain this one more time, sweetheart, because clearly the words ain't registering. You're mine. I'm yours."

She sighs. "I know. It's just... how are we going to make this work? I've never tried long distance before. And I've seen firsthand how those girls throw themselves at fighters. Being away and all that temptation... It sounds like the perfect recipe for heartache. It's why... It's why I tried to end this before either of us got hurt—mostly me."

I release her face and pull her hand closer. I place a soft kiss on her knuckles and rub it in, making it as permanent as I can. "Since you looked me up, I'm assuming you heard about my injury."

"Yes." She sniffles. "That's another thing. I saw the footage and read the reports. I don't think I could handle watching you get hurt again. I always struggled when I had to patch up Killian in the early days. And that was just Kill. And you're, well, you know, *you.*"

A smile spreads across my face. "I came here to talk to Killian. Ever since my injury, things just haven't been the same in the ring. I used to be fearless. Now... now, I hesitate like a little bitch."

"Hey, there is nothing weak when it comes to worrying about your own wellbeing. I'd actually be more concerned if it hadn't impacted you."

"In the ring, hesitancy will cost you the fight. All it takes is one second of self-doubt to get your ass knocked out." I gulp, thinking about my last match. I was almost KO'd by a sucker punch. Fortunately, I regained my senses quickly enough. But I made it by the skin of my teeth. I know it. And so do the coaches. "I wanted to ask how Killian did it. How he transitioned from a life in the ring to one in his hometown. I've never been good at anything other than fighting. It's all I've ever known. Growing up in a boys home, you have to get tough, fast, or they'll eat you alive."

"I had no idea." I shake my head at her concern.

"It's water under the bridge, sweetheart. It's just... walking away from all you know, it isn't easy. Even if it's for your own wellbeing. At least,

I thought the choice was difficult, until I met you."

"Me?"

My cock springs to action as her pale skin pinkens. "Yes, you. Don't ask me to explain it. Because I can't. But the moment I laid eyes on you, everything else fell away. When I think of my future now, all I can see is you."

"This is crazy," she says in disbelief.

"Crazy or not, it's the truth. Look, I know this is fast. But I guess that makes sense. I've never been conventional in any other aspects of my life. I don't know why I'd start now. We can take things slow." She laughs. "You know what I mean. I want you, all of you. Nothing else. If you're not ready for me to move in with you, I'll get an apartment nearby. I've already talked to Killian about training people at his gym. Help shape the future fighters."

"You'd move here? Just like that."

"Give up my overpriced studio apartment in Atlantic City, which is primarily used for storage? To come live here and see you as much as possible? It's a no-brainer. Before my injury, I was always training or traveling. I never bothered establishing roots anywhere. Never wanted to. Until now."

Her eyes search mine. I sense she has several more questions, which is understandable. But we have the rest of our lives to work out the finer details.

"Hey, baby." I turn to see a man standing at the

edge of our table. *Who the fuck is he? And why the fuck is he calling my girl "baby"?*

Anita

CHAPTER TEN

*S*hit, shit, shit. *What the fuck is he doing here?* I risk a glance at Declan. His knuckles are white as he clenches them tighter. "What are you doing here?" I ask Steve.

He gives me a smile I used to believe was charming. "You didn't answer my call, baby. We need to talk." He shoots a nasty look to Declan before turning back to me. "Privately."

"The fuck you are," Declan roars as he stands. He easily towers over Steve's six-foot stature by a good few inches. Where Declan is solid and bulky muscle, Steve is lean and trim. He is athletic, and so drastically different.

I place my palm on Declan's flexing arm and attempt to calm him down. "It's okay, I can handle

Declan looks at Killian, who's standing behind Steve while preparing to handle any sudden altercation. Killian shakes his head in return. Declan then glances at me before letting out a huff and sinking back into the booth. Steve misinterprets the situation, not realizing how close he is to having his face pounded in by two professional fighters. Given we grew up together, he knows about Killian—every local does. But he is under the illusion that because they were once schoolyard chums, he's exempt from getting his ass kicked. Killian's motto has always been: *family before all else.* We might not be blood. But in his eyes, I'm as much his family as his natural-born siblings.

"Let's get out of here." Steve reaches to grab my arm, and I turn from him.

"I'm not going anywhere with you," I seethe, crossing my arms over my chest while simultaneously creating as much distance as I can.

"Don't be that way, baby." As he leans closer, the alcohol on his breath assaults my senses. *Shit, this isn't good.* Steve is known for making bad choices when he's had too much to drink. During our senior party, he got drunk, and we had to spend the night keeping him from sitting in the bonfire. *God, why did I ever date him?*

"I'm not your baby, Steve. You made that perfectly clear when you dumped me. Now, please leave." As much as I am repulsed by him at the moment, I don't want him to get hurt. He's a douche. But I don't think he deserves the beating he's asking for.

"Baby, baby, baby. You misunderstood me," he slurs. "I said we needed some time apart. To think. I *thinked,* and now I want you to come back to me. We can get married and make babies."

"I'm not going to warn you again, Steve. Go home. Sleep it off. Then lose my number. We're over."

My ex looks between me and Declan. He narrows his gaze. "Seriously, you want this meathead over me." He hitches his thumb over his shoulder and points at Declan. "Real funny, Nita. Let's get going." This time, he grabs my wrist and attempts to pull me with him. I'm surprised and stumble. Two powerful arms catch me before I fall face-first to the floor.

Declan pulls me up into his embrace and tugs me close. "I got you, sweetheart."

"You fucking slut!" I turn to see Steve struggling against Killian's hold. His arm is twisted behind his back with his heels partially off the ground.

"Steve, bro, if you value your testies, shut-the-fuck-up," Killian warns. I'm surprised by his restraint. I guess he's become less hotheaded with age. Back in the day, he never would have given a warning before kicking someone's ass.

"No, man, she's a fucking slut. We broke up a week ago. And she's already riding someone else's dick." Steve's face is red as he yells, spit coming out with every other word. My heart clenches. I never imagined this sort of monster lived beneath the surface. He might be drunk and stupid, but that doesn't mean his feelings at the moment are untrue. Perhaps this is the most honest he's ever been with me. "Don't play stupid, Needy. Yeah, that's right, buddy. Do you know why we used to call her Needy Nita back in the day? Because this bitch always desperately needed someone's cock—"

I see red. As natural as breathing, my hands instinctively fall to his shoulders and my knee rises to collide with his groin. As he lurches forward, my fist pulls back and makes a sick crunching sound before blood sprays. I cradle my wrist and watch Killian drag Steve out the front door.

"Shit, let me look at that." Declan inspects my hand. I hiss as he applies pressure to one of my knuckles. "I don't think it's broken. But we should get you bandaged up, and put some ice on it."

My eyes burn as tears leak out. "Some date, huh?"

Declan laughs and wipes the moisture from my cheeks. "It was fucking amazing."

"Seriously? You still want this?" I gesture to myself, knowing I must look like a crazed hot mess.

"Sweetheart..." He cups my cheek. "I never thought a chick kneeing a guy in the balls before breaking his nose would turn me on. But... here we are." He pulls me closer, allowing me to feel exactly how the encounter affected him. "Let's get you cleaned up, yeah? Then, afterwards, I'm going to help ease all your aches and pains."

And just like that, my hand no longer hurts as the tension in my core overpowers my senses.

"Here." Sean tosses us a bag of ice. "You guys better scram. The cops will be here any minute. And based on the way y'all are fucking each other with your eyes right now, I'd hate for you two to get arrested for indecent exposure, on top of everything else."

Declan scoops me up, bridal-style. Not wasting another moment, he grabs our stuff, rushes out of the bar, and carries me the few blocks home. I'm so consumed by everything Declan I don't even bother to look around and see how Killian is handling Steve. None of it matters. All that matters is us. It might be fast and crazy. *But when it's right, it's right.* And nothing in my entire life has felt more right than being in his arms.

Faster than I thought, he has us through my apartment door and in my bedroom. He gently lays me down on my bed and retreats into the bathroom. Moments later, he returns with my med kit before squatting in front of me. He takes my hand in his and carefully removes the icepack from my fist. Then, grabbing one of my alcohol swabs, he looks at me. "This is going to sting." I hiss as he cleans the wound. After he bandages my hand, he places a soft kiss on top. "Does it still hurt?" he asks as his fingers trace down my thighs.

I nod. "So bad."

He quirks an eyebrow. "You know the best remedy for pain... is distraction."

Leaning back, I lift my midsection as he slides my leggings over my hips. His nose hovers close to the apex of my thighs, his warm breath making me hotter by the second. With a heavy pant, he inhales my arousal. Declan hooks his thumbs in the waistband of my underwear before looking up at me, his eyes bright. Clear. *Determined.*

"I think I'm in love with you," he confesses, as he slides the cotton fabric down and tosses it to the floor.

I freeze, surprised. It's soon, probably too soon. And frankly, this is fucking insane. But the craziest part of it all is none of it actually scares me. It should... However, when he spoke those words, it was the most honest thing anyone has ever said to me.

My body jolts as he sucks my clit between his teeth. I use my good hand, grasp his hair, and hold him close. Skillfully, with his tongue and fingers, he pushes me to climax. "I love you too," I scream as my orgasm peaks. *God, I fucking love him.*

Declan

EPILOGUE

One year later

I pocket my lighter after igniting the last candle. Looking around, I take a final inventory.

Candles, check.

Flowers, check.

Wine, check.

Dinner... I glance at the oven. Check.

Lastly...

The jingle of her keys pulls me from my thoughts. *Shit, she's early.* I rush to the entryway, to intercept her before she walks in. The door hasn't even clicked shut and I'm already on her.

"Declan." She laughs as I cover her eyes with my hands and pull her back, close to my chest. "What are you doing?"

"I have a surprise for you." I lean forward and whisper in her ear. And the little minx that she is, Anita grinds her ass into my cock.

"I told you I didn't want to do—"

I shush her. "Please, sweetheart. Let me right this wrong. You deserve this." My chest puffs out with pride as she melts into me. True to my word, over the past year, I have worked diligently to right every wrong she's ever experienced. I always thought being a boyfriend would be difficult. That I'd screw it up somehow. I'm starting to think it seemed like a lot of work because it wasn't for the right person. With Anita, I never doubt myself. I never hesitate. Even during the few times we've argued—it's bound to happen in all good relationships—it still feels right. Well, at least the make-up sex does. Occasionally, I'll pick a stupid argument just to fuck her silly. She loves it.

Like tonight. She told me she didn't want to do anything special for Valentine's Day. *That every day was about showing how much we love each other. There was no need for some socially pressured, commercial holiday. Today was just a Friday, like any other week.* Although I get what she's saying and agree with most of it, that doesn't mean I don't want to show her how much I love her. As she mentioned, we show it every day. Why should today be any different? It's just a tad more extravagant than usual. I know my girl though. To her liking, we are staying home.

With her eyes still covered, I lead her into the living room. "Are you ready?"

"Yes," she whispers. I can already feel her body vibrate with excitement.

"Open," I demand as I remove my hands.

Her gasp is worth all the work I put in today, in order to get her out of the house. Granted, convincing her to go see Tiffany and the baby isn't that difficult. Still, there were a lot of small things that had to go just right to make tonight perfect. "You did this all for me?" She leans back into my chest.

I snag my arms around her waist and rest my chin on her head. "Anything for you. Come on, take a seat." I lead her to the table and pull her chair out, like the gentleman I am. Off to the kitchen, I return moments later with two covered plates. I place them at their designated settings and then remove her lid.

"Did you get these from KO's?" She chuckles at the burger and fries.

"Only the best for you," I say with a cheeky grin.

"You are pulling out all the stops tonight, aren't you? Are you trying to pamper me, hoping to sway me to do butt stuff?" She raises a suspicious brow.

I snatch a fry from her plate and shrug my shoulders as I eat her forbidden food. *As if I need to persuade her.* Her grin is all the confirmation I need. We both know if we wanted to venture outside of the norm, she wouldn't need the bribery. Another sign proving that when you're with the right person, it's easy. I always assumed you'd get bored with the same old sex in a relationship. *Variety was the spice of life.* But the truth is, guys, when she loves and trusts you, more doors than you could ever imagine open up. *Oh, the things we've tried...* I adjust myself at the thought. The best part? Most of the crazy stuff has been her idea.

It didn't take long for me to learn what really drew us together. Both of us grew up without traditional families. Anita, with a single mom, who was never around. And me, in the system, until I aged out. We both created our own makeshift families. However, as the years pass, they're no longer enough. Because we grow up... We fall out of touch. We get married. Have children. Move away. In a sea of loneliness, we found each other. And now, we both have everything we've ever wanted, even if some of us (me) never really admitted it. We have someone to love and be there—by our side.

While eating dinner, we catch up on the week. Although she doesn't work nearly as many hours since she switched to a local private practice, occasionally, we have weeks where we only see each other briefly before bed. More recently, I've been working overtime, helping one of my guys prepare for his first title fight, and she's been volunteering at a local clinic to ease the overflow.

Brandishing her final fry, she wipes up the last bit of sauce from her plate. Once she's finished, I stand and take her hand. She moves to clear the table, but I pull her to follow me instead.

"I'll take care of it later." I lead her to the center of the dark, candlelit living room. "Alexa, play Valentine's Playlist."

A second later, the first song streams through the speakers.

She wraps her arms around my neck and looks up at me. "This is beautiful. Thank you." With a content sigh, she rests her head on my chest as we sway to the slow beat. "Can we stay like this forever?" she whispers.

I squeeze her tighter. "That's the plan." She pulls back slightly and studies my face. Taking advantage of the song's finale, I hold one of her hands and drop to a knee. The flames from the candles reflect on the tears building in her eyes. "Anita, I used to think there was nothing more to life than the octagon. That nothing could satisfy me the way the thrill of the fight did. I never realized how empty my life was until I met you. You keep me on my toes, like it's a title fight and I'm tied in the fifth round, and the bells are about to sound. You're my everything." I pull the ring from my pocket and present it to her. "Will you marry me?"

"Yes," she exclaims, without hesitation. I slide the band on her finger and scoop her up into my arms, devouring her cries of joy. I will never tire of kissing her. I won several championship titles during my career. But none were as fulfilling as the one naming me her husband.

The end

Cassie

EXPECTING MOORE: SNEAK PEEK

February 9th

"Ouch," I hiss, sucking the blood from my finger. The stupid thorn got me, and not for the first time today. This is flipping pathetic. Here I am—again—back living with my parents, helping at their flower shop and stuck making floral arrangements for a bridal shower. *White roses, how cliché?* I don't mean to be catty; honestly, the arrangement is beautiful. It's just... right now, the last thing I want to do or look at is anything related to a wedding. Which is weird coming from me—I love weddings. I've been planning my own for as long as I can remember. But after recent events, the last thing I'm thinking about is getting married.

"*Níl ach braon beag fola ort.*" My father chuckles, handing me a cloth to wrap around my finger.

While the man immigrated to the United States almost forty years ago, he still enjoys teasing me in his native Irish tongue.

"Da, it is more than a little blood." I wave my finger at him. Only a small droplet trickles down—I'm obviously being a little overdramatic. But being the baby of our family and his only daughter, I play it up as much as possible. Even though I'm almost thirty, he still likes to view me as his little girl.

"*Próseche.* You are getting blood on the arrangements, Cassandra." Thanks to my unique heritage, I am fluent in English, Gaelic, and Greek. My mother's Greek heritage is the only reason I do not have a traditional Irish name like my brothers. While Da thinks my little antics are cute, they don't work as well on my mother.

"Sorry, Ma." I rush to clean and wrap my bleeding finger. When I turn back around, my mother is picking apart my arrangement and undoing all my work. I love her—she's my mother, after all—but she can be extremely nit-picky. Then again, when it comes to floral arrangements, she is a genuine artist. Numbers, math, have always been my thing. Burying myself in endless piles of data and spreadsheets calms and centers me. Flowers do that for her. Although she is proud of my education, I believe she still resents the fact I didn't inherit her gifts. None of us did. That didn't stop her from trying to make me the best florist she could. I think she assumed that, being her daughter, it would come naturally to me—*it didn't.* Sure, I am able to put together an arrangement or two, but I don't have the instinct that she does.

Ma sighs, pulling blood-stained roses from the arrangement and tossing them into the trash. "Cassandra, head home. Get cleaned up. I will finish up the order and we will meet you later tonight." She dismisses me, her brow scrunched in frustration as she figures out how to salvage the mess I've made.

Yup, my mother just politely kicked me out of the shop—again. Giving my parents each a brief kiss, I bundle up to face the freezing Minnesota winter. Although it's so cold my nostrils stick together when I take in a breath, I wouldn't want to live anywhere else. I was made for this weather.

ᘯᘍᘯᘍᘯᘍᘯᘍᘯ

Instead of going home, I stop at K.O. Murphy's, a pub my brother Killian owns. It is also conveniently within walking distance of my parents' house, which makes drinking here ideal. Not to mention, I mostly drink for free. I'm not a freeloader or anything; he just refuses to accept my money. I make sure to always tip everyone well to make up for the fact I don't have to pay. When he needs it, I volunteer to help wait tables. I might not be the best server, but it is a delightful distraction during times like these, where I'm not working and need something to do to keep myself from going mad.

Taking a seat at the bar, I flag down Sean, my brother's friend, who is also the lead bartender. "Hiya, Cassie, what can I get ya this evening?" Sean asks, his green eyes sparkling with the sort of mischief that matches his tone.

"Seriously, Sean? I am a little hurt you even need to ask." I feign insult, playing along with his game. Sean already knows what I want to drink. I've been drinking here almost exclusively for five years—ever since my brother opened the place after he retired from fighting.

Giving me his token flirty grin, he pours me a Murphy's Irish Stout. Yeah, given our family name and heritage, my brother has coined the Murphy's branding as much as possible. Even if the beer hadn't been created by a distant ancestor, it would still be my drink of choice. While Guinness is delicious, I feel this smooth drink doesn't get the attention it deserves. I take a sip of my beer and enjoy the mild coffee flavor. Glancing around, I notice that the place is packed, which isn't surprising for a Friday night. Thankfully, while busy, it doesn't feel overcrowded like other places. Maybe that is because I know almost everyone here?

"What kind of trouble are you planning tonight?" Sean teases while wiping down the bar.

"Just the usual," I toss back before giving him my most sinister smile. "World domination."

He lifts his chin, gesturing to someone behind me. "I am sure if anyone could do it, you two could."

Before I have a chance to turn around, I feel two thin arms wrap around me from behind, hugging my waist. "Hey, Cassie," Moira, my best friend, says. Squeezing me tight before sliding onto the bar stool next to me, she removes her jacket, revealing a cream blouse—her naturally vibrant red hair pulled back into a tight bun. She came here straight from the office. *Ugh, how I miss having an office to go to.* Moira lets out a deep sigh before offering me a soft smile. Ever since the breakup, she has been walking on eggshells around me. I really wish she would stop. "So how are you holding up?" Before taking off to help other patrons, Sean slides Moira a Guinness (because we haven't been able to convert her yet) and brings us some appetizers.

I roll my eyes at her question. "Fine, I guess. I am still looking for work. Hopefully I find something soon. I think Ma is going to kill me if I mess up another one of her arrangements."

Moira snort-laughs into her beer. Growing up alongside me, Moira knows my mother well and is aware of how particular she is about her flowers, and how she isn't afraid to show her disappointment in my lack of skillset. "I am sure someone will get back to you soon. You have only been looking for a few weeks."

"Yeah, it's just... I need to get back to work. I'm going crazy without my numbers. I need purpose." I pout and then toss a pretzel bite into my mouth, savoring the salt and warm cheese.

"Oh, speaking of jobs, guess who I talked to

the other day?" Moira yells excitedly over the music, "Tilly!"

I smile, thinking of my old college roommate and friend. I feel bad for not keeping in touch with her. But that is life after college. You mean well, but eventually you all break off and go your separate ways. It doesn't help that Tilly refuses to use Facebook—or any social media for that matter—and lives almost two hours from me. "I haven't heard from her in forever. How's she doing?"

"Good, I guess." Moira's eyes tear up and her voice breaks a little as she speaks. "Her parents actually passed away a few months ago."

"Oh, wow, that is awful. I had no idea." I take a swig of my drink, trying to wash away the foul taste of guilt I feel. I can't believe she has been going through such a hardship and I knew nothing about it. Well, I guess Moira didn't either. Unfortunately, that doesn't stop me from being remorseful over not being there for my friend.

"Yeah, it sounds like she is doing better though. Tilly actually got married a couple of weeks ago," Moira says, then immediately retreats, knowing marriage has been a sore subject for me more recently.

"It's okay, Moira. I appreciate you looking out for me. But I need to move past this. I am happy that she got married." No lie, I am happy for her. It pains me a little, and I find myself a tad jealous. But I don't want to become one of those people who can't celebrate my friend's happiness, just because things are not so great for me right now.

"I know. I am sorry..." Moira clears her throat. "Also, she's pregnant."

"That's exciting. We should plan on visiting her soon. Or maybe invite her up here and take her out shopping for the baby," I offer, trying to heal some of the hurt and guilt in my heart. "I'm confused. What does this have to do with a job?"

"Actually, she called looking to see if I knew anyone in need of work."

"Oh yeah, she looking for someone to help at the bookshop?" That would make sense, needing some extra help with a baby on the way. Running a business isn't a simple forty hour a week gig. Knowing Tilly as well as I do, while she loves the shop, she wouldn't want to be gone from her child that much.

"I guess it is helping her brother out. He needs someone at his auto shop, to manage his books and stuff." Moira takes a quick drink. "I couldn't really think of anyone looking right now, well, except for you. Unfortunately, you'd have to relocate to Tral Lake—so I didn't think it would be something you'd be interested in. If you can think of anyone though, you should pass it along. Apparently, her brother is super nervous about letting a stranger come in and manage his books."

"Which one?" I try to recall her siblings. Who

was it that was the mechanic?

"Her eldest brother." Moira pauses for a moment, tapping her chin. "Robbie."

I nod. "Ah, okay, I never met him. I really only ever met Jake, all those times he came to visit campus, and Scott at graduation."

Moira giggles, thinking of Jake. "If Jake needed an office manager, I would quit my job in a heartbeat." We both laugh. Jake was super hot. I'm sure he still is. The guy totally seeped sex pheromones from his pores. Tilly is drop-dead gorgeous, without even trying. She never needed makeup or anything else. She is just naturally stunning. Yeah, Jake, being her twin, inherited all those same qualities. I swear anytime he came to campus, I could hear the girls' panties drop as he walked by.

Goofing off, Moira and I continue to drink our beers and chat at the bar. Since the breakup, it's been nice getting to hang out with my best friend. It feels like forever since we have been able to do this—just the two of us. Eventually, we hit the drunk state of the evening, where we feel the need to pose for selfies at the bar and post them to Facebook. Scrolling through the newsfeed, we laugh at the comments our friends are leaving when something catches my eye. Moira notices and snatches the phone from me.

"Let it go, Cassie," she yells, turning her back to me and blocking the phone with her body.

"Moira, give me the darn phone," I chide. She

looks down at the screen with a frown before huffing and passing it back to me. Studying the post, I can't help but feel the broken pieces of my heart shatter more.

"Come on, Cassie, you're better than him. He did you a favor, if you ask me," Moira pleads, trying to prevent the train wreck that is happening in my head.

"Sorry, Moira. I need to get going," I say, throwing a twenty down for Sean. Getting up, I run smack dab into a firm chest.

"Whoa, Cassie. Where ya heading off to?" Killian asks, his smile quickly turning to a frown as he notices the look of anguish on my face. "Hey, what happened?" Killian glances between Moira and me. "Did some drunk asshole try something?" He then cracks his knuckles, prepared to beat up one of his patrons if necessary.

"No, Kill, it's fine. I'm tired. I'll catch you both later," I say, walking away quickly and pulling my jacket snug around me. Off in the distance, I can hear Killian asking Moira details about what happened. I don't stick around to listen to the conversation because it doesn't matter. I need to get away from here. I love my family, and Moira, but right now everything reminds me of *him. I need to do something.* I don't even take a second to reconsider before grabbing my phone and calling my old friend. "Hey, Tilly, it's Cassie."

"Cassie? Oh, hi. How are you? I feel like we haven't spoken in ages." Tilly sounds excited and happy on the other end of the line. That is what I want to be again. I want to be happy, not constantly reminded of my heartbreak. How is it ever supposed to heal when the wound keeps getting picked at?

"I am doing good. I'm sorry for calling late, but I was actually just at the bar with Moira—she mentioned you were looking for someone to help at your brother's shop?"

THANK YOU

Thank you for reading Flirty At Murphy's: A Murphy's Bar Novella. I hope you enjoyed reading this story as much as I did writing it.

Keep reading Expecting Moore, the second book in my Moore Family Series on Amazon. It's available for free with Kindle Unlimited. Check it out here:

A special thank you to my amazing editor and friend Kat Pagan, with Pagan Proofreading. Without your keen eye for detail and ability to understand what I am trying to say better that I can sometimes, I know my books wouldn't be nearly as special without your touch.

Thank you to Brittany and Savannah for beta reading for me once again. Your review and feedback are always greatly appreciated. Especially when I am asking you both to read something last minute.

Dahlia, you rock. I feel like no more words are needed than that.

Daria, thank you again for all your guidance when it comes to my designing and marketing. Your eye for design is spectacular, and you help me take everything to the next level.

MORE BY FRANKIE PAGE

The Moore Family Series:
· Forever Moore (Tilly and Jax)
· Expecting Moore (Robbie and Cassie)
· Want You Moore (Jake)... TBD 2022
· Moore Family Book 4 (Scott)... TBD

The Murphy Brothers:
· Flirty at Murphy's: A Murphy's Bar Novella
· Murphy Brothers Book 1 (Killian)... TBD
· Murphy Brothers Book 2 (Cian)... TBD

Rose's Inferno Trilogy:
· Retribution (Book 1)
· Rose's Inferno Trilogy Book 2... TBD 2022
· Rose's Inferno Trilogy Book 3... TBD 2022

Standalone Novella:
· Learning to Love Again

LET'S KEEP IN TOUCH

Visit my website and learn more about my books, sign up for my newsletter, and follow me on all my social media platforms:

Manufactured by Amazon.ca
Acheson, AB